What Are Friends For?

For David – S.G.

For Jackie – P.D.

KINGFISHER
An imprint of Larousse plc
New Penderel House, 283-288 High Holborn
London WC1V 7HZ

First published in paperback by Kingfisher 1998
2 4 6 8 10 9 7 5 3 1
First published in hardback by Kingfisher 1998

Text copyright © Sally Grindley 1998
Illustrations copyright © Penny Dann 1998

A CIP catalogue record for this book
is available from the British Library.

ISBN 0 7534 0290 4

Printed in Hong Kong

What Are Friends For?

Sally Grindley

Illustrated by Penny Dann

KING*f*ISHER

Jefferson Bear and Figgy Twosocks went
walking one day in the sunny green woods.
   "JB," asked Figgy Twosocks,
"are you my friend?"

"Yes," said Jefferson Bear. "I am your friend, and you are my friend."

"But what is a friend for?" asked Figgy Twosocks.

"Well…" said Jefferson Bear. "A friend is for playing."

"Goody," said Figgy Twosocks. "Let's play hide-and-seek."

"All right," said Jefferson Bear. "You hide first."

Figgy Twosocks hid in a hollow tree.

Jefferson Bear looked everywhere,

but couldn't find her.

When it was his turn,
he hid behind a tree stump.
Figgy Twosocks
found him straightaway.
    "You're better at this
than me," said
Jefferson Bear.

"I'll help you this time,"
said Figgy Twosocks. She hid
under a pile of leaves,
but left the tip of her
tail showing.

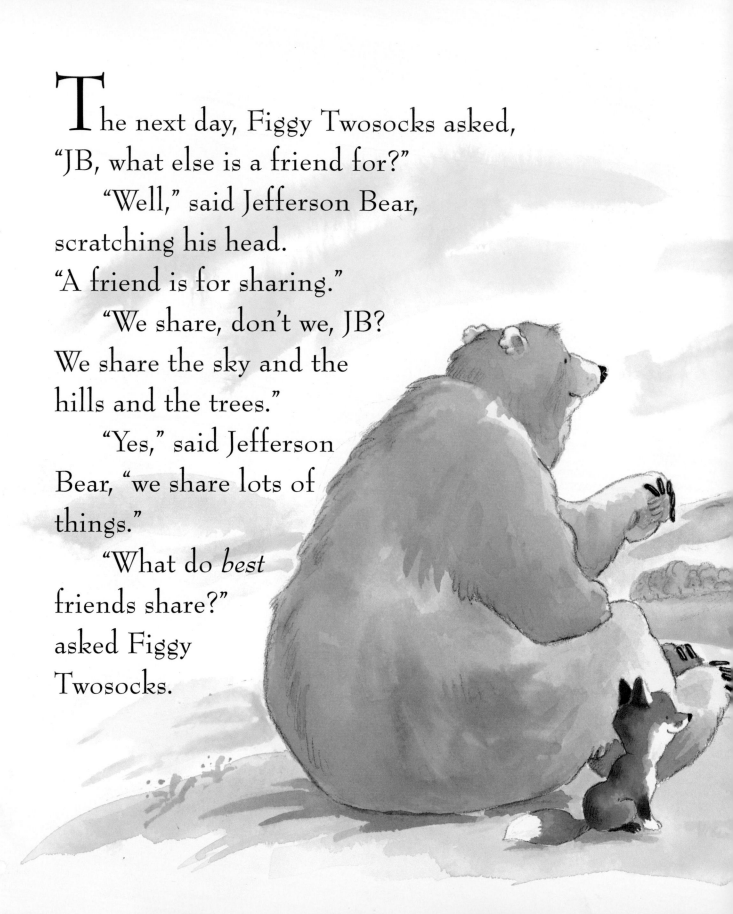

The next day, Figgy Twosocks asked, "JB, what else is a friend for?"

"Well," said Jefferson Bear, scratching his head. "A friend is for sharing."

"We share, don't we, JB? We share the sky and the hills and the trees."

"Yes," said Jefferson Bear, "we share lots of things."

"What do *best* friends share?" asked Figgy Twosocks.

"Well," said Jefferson Bear,
"best friends share their favourite things."
Figgy Twosocks thought about this, then darted
off through the woods. When she came back,
she was tugging an enormous
bramble covered with
blackberries.

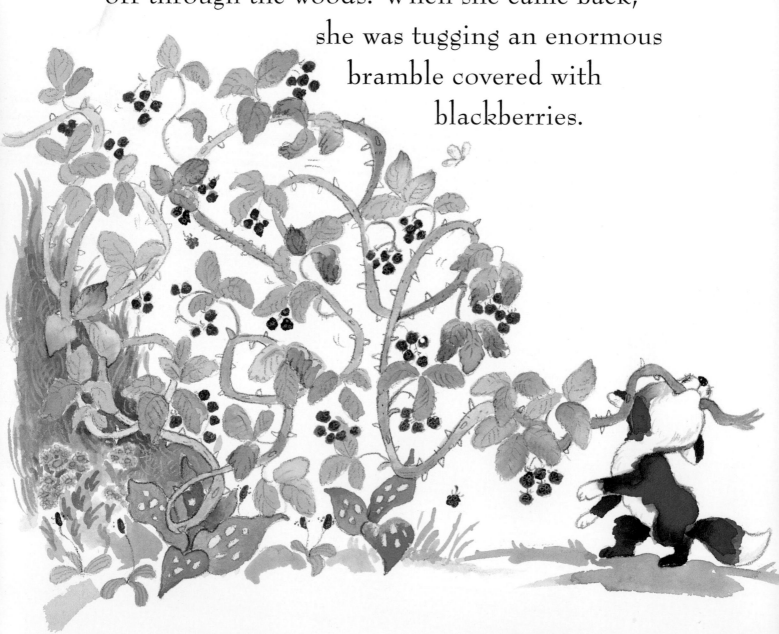

"Would you like some, JB?"
she said. "Blackberries
are my favourites.
Yummy, aren't they?"

"De–licious," said Jefferson Bear.

That afternoon, loud squeals woke
Jefferson Bear from his sleep.

yelp! yelp! yelp! yelp!

yelp! yelp! yelp! yelp!

"I'm coming," he bellowed.
"What's the matter?"

He found Figgy Twosocks lying on the ground.

"You've got a thorn in your foot. Keep still and I'll take it out."

"Will it hurt?" whimpered Figgy Twosocks.

"I'll be as gentle as I can," said Jefferson Bear.

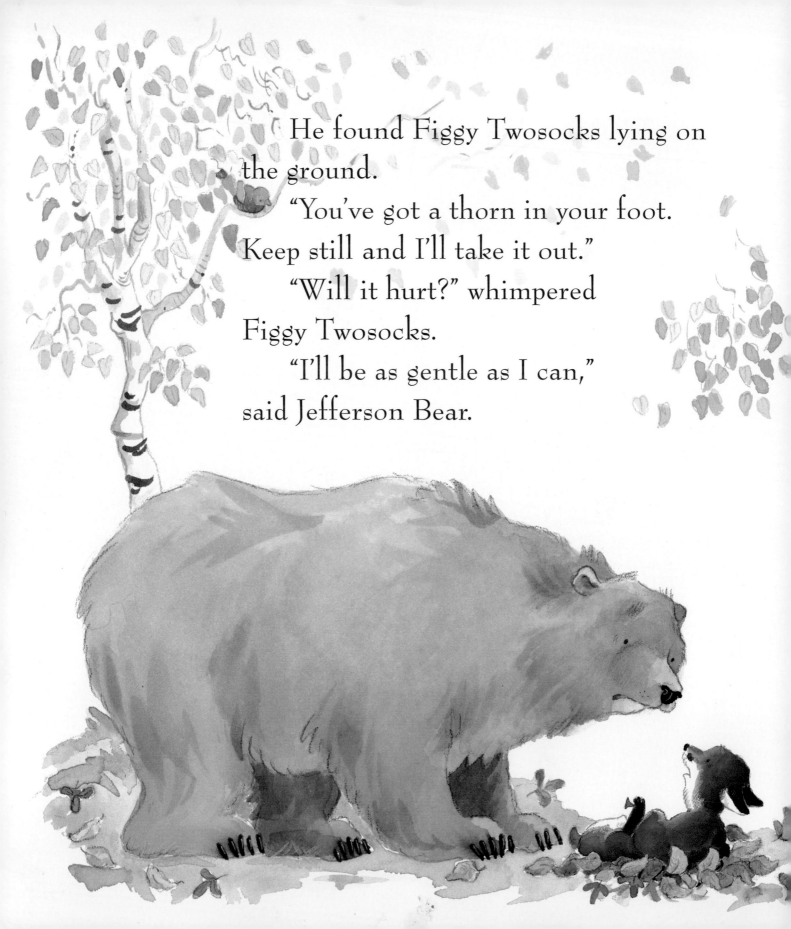

Figgy Twosocks was frightened when she saw her friend's sharp teeth, but she lay still. Jefferson Bear closed his teeth round the thorn and pulled.

As soon as it was out, Figgy Twosocks jumped up and pranced around.

"Thank you, JB," she said.
"Thank you for helping me."
"That's what friends are for,"
said Jefferson Bear.

The next afternoon, Jefferson Bear was dozing
in the sun. Figgy Twosocks wanted to play.
She crept up behind him and yelled...

Jefferson Bear nearly jumped out of his
wobbly fur. Figgy Twosocks ran round and round
squealing, "Made you jump! Made you jump!"
and laughed and waved her tail.

Jefferson Bear
didn't think it was funny.

"Go away, Figgy Twosocks," he said.
"You have made me cross."

"But I want to play," said Figgy Twosocks.

"And I want to sleep," said Jefferson Bear.
"A big brown bear needs his sleep."

"And a little red fox needs her play,"
said Figgy Twosocks.

"Then go and play somewhere else,"
said Jefferson Bear.

"You're not my friend any more," said
Figgy Twosocks sadly, and she trudged off.

When Jefferson Bear woke up next morning,
he felt sorry he had upset his friend.

"I'll play with her today," he said to himself.

But Figgy Twosocks stayed away.

Jefferson Bear began to worry. He went to
her den and called, "Figgy Twosocks,
it's Jefferson Bear.
Are you all right?"

There was no reply.

Jefferson Bear's worry grew. He walked to
the edge of the river and called again,
"Where are you, Figgy Twosocks?"

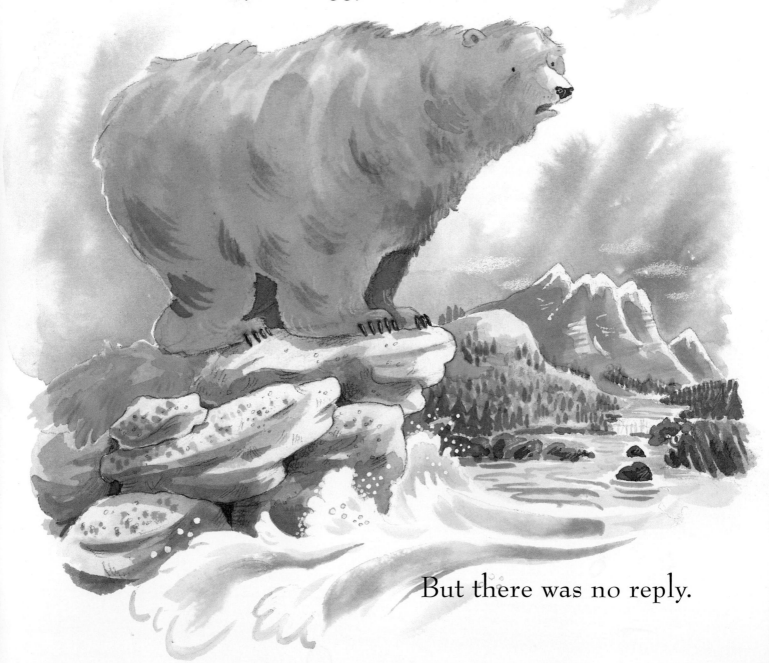

But there was no reply.

Jefferson Bear's worry grew bigger. He walked through the woods calling, "Come out, Figgy Twosocks, it's me, Jefferson Bear."

But there was still no reply.

At last, he came to the hollow tree where
they had played hide-and-seek. He saw the tip
of a tail sticking out.

"Figgy Twosocks, is that you?"
he called. "It's JB."

He listened and thought he heard something.

He listened again and was sure he heard a sniff.

The sniff grew louder and louder and louder until it turned into a **great**

big

SOB.

"Figgy Twosocks?" said Jefferson Bear.
"Yes," sobbed Figgy Twosocks.
"Please come out," said Jefferson Bear.
"I miss you."

"I'm sorry, JB," said Figgy Twosocks.
"I didn't mean to make you cross."

"And I'm sorry I was so grumpy,"
said Jefferson Bear. "Let's go and play."

"JB," sniffed Figgy Twosocks,
"does that mean you're still my friend?"

"Of course I'm still your friend,"
said Jefferson Bear. "A friend is for ever."